QUICK

BLACKOUT

ANNE SCHRAFF

SADDLEBACK
EDUCATIONAL PUBLISHING

QUICKREADS

SADDLEBACK
EDUCATIONAL PUBLISHING
www.sdlback.com

ISBN-13: 978-1-61651-190-6
ISBN-10: 1-61651-190-7
eBook: 978-1-60291-912-9

Printed in Guangzhou, China
0310/03-20-10

15 14 13 12 11   1 2 3 4 5

■ ■ ■

Brevin McCoy was on a roll. He was earning great sales commissions at a fine men's clothing store and taking college classes at night. Just recently, he'd moved into his own apartment. His life couldn't have been better—until the night of Nealy Hamm's party.

Anything and everything was happening there. As the action got wilder, Brevin felt like going home. It really wasn't his kind of scene at all. But he had stayed. Then someone slipped a dangerous designer drug into his soda, and he'd ended up in the emergency room. The aftereffects had been serious—*very* serious. In fact, they ended

Brevin's life as he had known it. He had spent two months in a convalescent hospital, going through terrifying flashbacks almost every day.

Now he was back living in his parents' house—his job gone, his car about to be repossessed. He was 20 years old and starting over again. He might as well be 18 and fresh out of high school.

Worst of all, a lot of people in the neighborhood were calling him 'Wacko McCoy' behind his back. That night at the party, he'd gone ballistic. It had taken three paramedics to restrain him. So now he was the butt of snide jokes. And since he got home, he hadn't heard a word from his girlfriend, Alyssa.

Brevin went to the phone to call her. He figured he'd probably get the answering machine again. It seemed to be Alyssa's way of avoiding him.

But this time Alyssa answered. Brevin couldn't believe how nervous he felt. Before the drug episode, he had always been so self-confident. Now his voice came out an octave higher than normal. "Hi, Alyssa," he stammered. "This is Brevin. Would you—uh—like to catch a movie tonight? If you've got other plans, that's all right—but, hey, if you aren't doing anything, you know—" Brevin got ready for the rebuff that he was sure was coming.

But Alyssa sounded friendly. "Hi, Brev. I'm just doing a crossword puzzle," she said. "I'd love to get out to a movie."

Brevin broke out in a big smile. This was the first good thing that had happened to him since he got home from the convalescent home.

■ ■ ■

Alyssa was ready and waiting when Brevin got there. She looked beautiful in her white slacks and red pullover. He'd half-forgotten how great-looking she was. "Hey, it's really good to see you, girl," Brevin said, giving her an awkward little hug.

"I missed you, too, Brevin," Alyssa said sweetly. "It's been a long time."

"I called you a couple of times," Brevin began, but then he was sorry for even bringing that up. He didn't want to fault Alyssa for being cautious. He knew there was a lot of talk about him being crazy.

"My schedule has been just frantic," Alyssa said. "Grandma got sick and was in the hospital, and then I had to have a wisdom tooth pulled. But everything has settled down now. What about you, Brevin? Got a job yet?"

"I have some good leads," Brevin said. But that wasn't quite true. He was angling for a couple of going-nowhere jobs he wouldn't have even considered before all this happened.

"That's good," Alyssa said cheerfully. "You're looking fine, Brevin."

"Thanks," Brevin said. "You look terrific."

"I'm so glad you're better," Alyssa said. "Whoever put that drug in your drink ought to be in jail. What a creepy, evil thing to do! I never did trust that Nealy Hamm and his crowd of losers."

"Yeah. That drug really messed with my mind," Brevin said.

Alyssa nodded sympathetically. "Boy, after what happened to you, I'm not drinking *anything* at a party that doesn't come out of a sealed bottle!"

"Good idea," Brevin said, slowing for a pedestrian who was darting across the street. Then he spotted some of his old high school acquaintances on a street corner. They were the kind of guys who liked to bring other people down. To really get going, all they needed was a poor freshman who'd broken out in zits. They'd make his life *miserable!*

"Hey," Donnie Baker shouted when Brevin stopped his car for the light. "Alyssa— ain't you scared riding with Wacko McCoy? From what I hear, ol' Brev could freak out anytime."

Brevin looked straight ahead and pretended he didn't hear Donnie's insult.

"Don't mind fools like that," Alyssa said. "Mama always says that empty wagons make the most noise." She flipped on the radio just been the person who harmed Ms. Revere?

Could that drug have indeed turned Brevin McCoy into a madman? Surely, he reasoned desperately, the doctors would have warned him if such a thing were possible!

Wouldn't they?

Brevin was glad the movie they had chosen was a comedy. For a couple of hours, it helped him forget about what had happened to Ms. Revere. Brevin had an especially warm spot in his heart for the dedicated teacher. Her patient tutoring had gotten him through science class and enabled him to graduate.

After the movie, Brevin and Alyssa stopped at a taco stand. Two girls who were a year behind them at Bethune High worked there. Brevin remembered that they had both played soccer on Bethune's championship team.

"Did you hear what happened to Ms. Revere?" Alyssa asked red-headed Judy Carson.

"Yeah," Judy said. "We just heard about it on the radio."

Judy looked at Brevin then. "Oh, hi, Brevin. Are you—uh—okay now?"

■ ■ ■

"Sure, I'm okay," Brevin said. Lucy Arthur, the other girl, looked at him suspiciously. She stared at Brevin as if he might freak out at any moment.

As Brevin and Alyssa walked away, Brevin heard Judy say, "I heard they had to keep him in a straitjacket!"

"Wow!" Lucy giggled.

Brevin and Alyssa carried their tacos and sodas to a booth. "Brevin," Alyssa said, patting his hand, "Don't let kids like that bother you. They're horrible gossips. Remember when we were at Bethune? Poor Ms. Revere tried so hard to bring their grades up—but all they wanted to do was gossip and pass notes. Those two are real losers. That's why they got kicked off the soccer team."

"Yeah, but they're only saying what most of the other people around here are thinking. I really lost it that night at the party, Alyssa.

They say I kicked holes in the wall. They say I even busted up furniture!" Brevin said.

"You couldn't help it, Brevin," Alyssa said. "That's all in the past now, okay?"

Brevin smiled and tried to enjoy the rest of the evening.

■ ■ ■

When Brevin got home that night, his mother was still up.

"Mom," Brevin said, "did you hear that somebody attacked Ms. Revere, my science teacher at Bethune High?"

"No, I haven't been listening to the radio," Mom said. "What happened to her? She's such a dear person!"

"Some guy in a mask busted into her classroom yesterday. He tied her up and terrorized her," Brevin said.

"How awful! What's this world coming to? A fine young woman like that—such an intelligent, good teacher and so com-passionate. I hope she wasn't hurt bad," Mom said.

"She wasn't hurt *physically*—but she's probably really shaken up," Brevin said. "Sometimes a mental injury is worse than a cut or a bruise."

Brevin knew what he was talking about. The "shadow effect" of that drug was still roaming through his mind like a deadly serpent, striking at will. His ordeal had been much worse than a beating would have been. The doctors had told Brevin that the body heals more quickly than the mind.

Mom's face looked sad. "We have got to send that young woman a big bouquet or something," she said.

More details of the attack came out the next day. A medium-sized intruder wearing a skeleton Halloween mask had entered Ms. Revere's classroom. Without speaking a word, he'd overpowered her, tying her up and gagging her with duct tape. Then he'd written a threatening message on the chalkboard.

SKELETON RULES, the message said. *REVERE IS DOOMED. REVERE SHALL BE A SKELETON, TOO.*

Brevin thought back to his own high school days. He couldn't remember any student who had ever been angry enough with Ms. Revere to harm her. Maybe Donnie Baker and his friends had tangled with her a few times. But she was always so helpful and respectful of every student. She was also very pretty. Most of the boys looked for excuses to talk to her.

■ ■ ■

Howard Meade came over that afternoon. He was Brevin's best friend since high school. He asked if Brevin wanted a part-time job at the car wash where Howard's kid brother worked. Brevin didn't want to work at a car wash with a bunch of teenagers. But he had to get money from somewhere. As he talked with Howard, the subject of Ms. Revere's attack came up.

"I bet she has a boyfriend, and maybe she jilted him and he did it," Howard said. "Remember that guy on a motorcycle she used to date?"

Brevin shook his head. "Nah. Ms. Revere is a class act, Howie. Even the motorcycle guy didn't seem to be *that* much of a creep!" he said.

Howard looked at his watch. "So, Brev, I gotta go. Do you want the car wash job or not? My brother can get you in, starting tomorrow. It's just minimum wage, but sometimes rich customers give good tips for doing an extra fine job. Once in a while my brother makes a nice piece of change," Howard said.

Brevin felt humiliated. "Your brother is just 16 years old, man!" he cried.

"Listen, I'm not pushing you to take the job," Howard said. "But if you're hurting for money, something is better than nothing!"

"Yeah, you're right," Brevin said. "Thanks, Howie. I'll take it."

He had always tried to pull his own weight. His mother was a nurse's aid at the hospital. She worked awfully hard for her modest paycheck. And Dad had been disabled by heart trouble.

"Mom," Brevin said that evening, "do you

remember the day before yesterday? I took a long nap in the afternoon. I guess I was still sleeping when you got home from work, huh?" Brevin needed to know that. If his mother had found him sleeping, he *couldn't* have been the guy who hurt Ms. Revere.

Mom smiled and shook her head. "That was Friday, right? No, baby, you weren't home when I got here. You'd gone off somewhere," she said. "It was already dark when you got home."

Oh, no! Brevin immediately broke into a cold sweat. He didn't remember going anywhere after his nap. He didn't remember a thing.

■ ■ ■

"Maybe I did do it," Brevin thought to himself. But why? Why? Brevin thought the world of that teacher.

Brevin trembled in panic. Maybe, he thought, he didn't *need* a reason. Maybe that terrible drug had been on the loose in his brain again, wreaking havoc with his

16

thinking—and now with his memory!

The next day Brevin reluctantly went to his car wash job. When he got out of his car, he ran into Donnie Baker and his friends. They were just hanging, idling the day away like they always did. All of them had dropped out of Bethune High. Not even Ms. Revere's mighty efforts could save them. After Donnie had quit school in his sophomore year, he did odd jobs. For a while he worked in an auto detailing shop. Before long, rumor had it that he had started dealing in stolen auto parts.

"Hey, here comes Wacko McCoy!" Donnie shouted. "Run for cover!"

One of the other boys, J.D. Land, was even nastier than Donnie. "Hey, man, you the one who messed up the teacher? They say it must have been a real crazy dude who did it. We think it sounds a lot like *you,* man." He laughed wildly at his own remark.

Brevin glared at J.D.'s smirking face. "That's a rotten lie! Ms. Revere was my favorite teacher at Bethune. I'd do anything for her," he cried.

"My girlfriend says you really lost it that night at Nealy's. She said you were busting up furniture and howling like a dog. Somebody like that could do anything," J.D. taunted. "Lucy said they had to lock you in an insane asylum."

"Lucy Arthur is a big-mouthed liar!" Brevin snapped.

Donnie laughed, enjoying Brevin's misery. "Lucy and Judy say you were acting real weird in the taco shop. They said Alyssa was real scared of you. They could tell she was wanting to get out of there real fast," he said.

"Oh, yeah? Well, that's another lie," Brevin said. By now he was sweating heavily.

"I bet you tied up that lady and scared her just for the fun of it," J.D. said. "Tell me, Wacko McCoy, just exactly what kind of things did you do to her?"

Brevin walked away. There was no way he could convince these guys of his innocence. They *wanted* to believe he was crazy. They would enjoy tormenting him no matter *what* they believed.

Brevin made a decision. After he finished work he would go to the taco stand. In a nice, polite way, he'd ask Judy and Lucy to stop spreading lies about him. Maybe they'd listen.

■ ■ ■

Mr. Wisinski, the car wash owner, complimented Brevin at the end of the day, saying he was the best guy who ever worked there. "You are very thorough and dependable," he said.

Brevin might have been pleased at the compliment, but he was four years older than the others. The teenagers were making fun of him. Brevin wanted to be back at his old job selling men's fine clothing. He had a knack for that. And the commissions were great.

Brevin wanted his old life back, but he was afraid. Maybe the Brevin McCoy he used to be had died of a drug overdose. Maybe a wild stranger would be occupying his mind from now on.

Brevin felt sick—sick and scared. *Everybody* seemed to be convinced that he was crazy and dangerous!

Even Brevin himself wasn't sure what the truth was.

■ ■ ■

That evening Howard came over. "You know what I think, man," Howard said. "I think Nealy Hamm did that to Ms. Revere."

"I don't know. Why would he want to mess with her?" Brevin asked.

"It's simple. She and another teacher at Bethune are working with the police on that new Neighborhood Watch program. They're urging people to be on the lookout for drug dealers and graffiti jocks and thieves. Nealy is into all that stuff. They never busted him for the drugs he took to that hip hop party. The rap is that he's selling drugs now. I think he wanted to send Ms. Revere a message. He wants her to be scared—real scared," Howard said. "Nealy Hamm wants the neighborhood left alone."

"Yeah, maybe," Brevin said. He really *wanted* to believe Howard's theory. "But how can we prove it?"

"Well, my cousin is a cop," Howard said. "When I see him, I'm gonna tell him my theory. Maybe the cops assigned to the case will put the heat on Hamm and come up with some proof."

"All right, man," Brevin said. What a relief it would be if they nabbed the guy who attacked Ms. Revere! It would stop people like Donnie and those yappy girls from gossiping.

■ ■ ■

On Saturday, Brevin took Alyssa to the beach. It was a cloudy, overcast day, and there weren't many people out. That suited Brevin fine. Since the drug overdose, he always felt a little nervous being around a crowd of people.

Alyssa sat on the beach towel and read a newspaper. When she opened the sports section, she said, "Look, Brevin. Keesha

Andrews helped the Bobcats win the college soccer championship. Remember Keesha in Ms. Revere's science class? She was a real scream. Remember when the rat got out?"

"Yeah," Brevin smiled. "Everybody was screaming, and Keesha just calmly grabbed the rat and put it back in the cage. Keesha was real tight with Lucy and Judy, wasn't she?"

"They all played soccer together. But Keesha kept her grades up, so she got the four-year college scholarship. Judy and Lucy spent too much time hanging at the mall. That's why they're making tacos now," Alyssa giggled.

"Alyssa," Brevin said suddenly, "Howie thinks he knows who hurt Ms. Revere. He's guessing it could be Nealy Hamm. Maybe Howie's onto something. Nealy hates it that Ms. Revere is trying to organize one of those neighborhood watch programs."

"Huh? Nealy Hamm? No way," Alyssa said with a laugh.

Brevin's spirits tumbled. "How come?"

he asked.

"Nealy is a big, chunky guy. Ms. Revere said her attacker had a medium build," Alyssa said.

"He could have gotten somebody to do his dirty work for him," Brevin said. "The word on the street is that Nealy is selling drugs big time. He's got the money to hire a goon."

"Nealy's not selling drugs," Alyssa scoffed. "He's a big blowhard. He's trying to make himself out to be this big bad dealer. But the truth is that he hasn't got two quarters to rub together. Think about it. He does odd jobs for his father to earn chump change!"

Brevin sank back on the sand, resting on his elbows. "Then who could have attacked Ms. Revere? Everybody liked her so much! Who would want to scare her like that? The poor woman could have had a fatal heart attack or something," Brevin said.

"Must have been some crazy person," Alyssa said. "That's all I can figure. You know—some demented weirdo who gets his kicks from scaring people."

■ ■ ■

Brevin knew that Alyssa would never hurt him on purpose. But her words felt like knives driving into his heart. After all, Brevin was the only "weirdo" in the neighborhood. He was the only one they called "wacko." Sure, there were some pretty strange homeless men around. But all those guys did was beg people for cigarette money. No one was afraid of them, because they weren't really crazy.

Brevin wouldn't share his private fears with Alyssa—or with anybody. But the horrifying question was still plaguing him. Had he awakened in the midst of a drug-crazed nightmare and attacked Ms. Revere?

"Brevin, what's wrong?" Alyssa said. "You look so sad."

"My life has sorta fallen apart, babe," Brevin said miserably.

"Yeah, I know—but you're only twenty!

You can enroll in community college next fall. Then you'll be right on track," Alyssa said.

"I've got a big blot on my record now, Alyssa," Brevin said.

"Brevin! Who could blame *you?* It wasn't *your* fault that somebody sneaked drugs into your soda and made you sick. That's just bad luck! It could have happened to anybody," Alyssa said.

"Yeah," Brevin said, "but it happened to me. It happened to Brevin McCoy—and the truth is that I'm not sure I can come back from it."

Brevin was feeling deeply depressed after he took Alyssa home. He buried his head in his hands. That was when the wild idea came to him. Why hadn't he thought of it before? Back in high school, when he was going through hard times, there was one person who always came through for him—Janice Revere.

Brevin knew what he had to do. He had to see her. He had to see his former teacher *right now.*

■ ■ ■

Brevin was shaking as he drove toward Ms. Revere's apartment. Lots of times she'd invited struggling students there for study sessions. Many a kid graduated because of those Saturday morning drills.

But now Brevin was afraid. Would Ms. Revere see him coming and call the police? Maybe by now she'd figured out for herself that he was the one who attacked her. Maybe it was only pity for his medical condition that had kept her from turning him in so far.

But Brevin was determined. He couldn't let his fears stop him.

He hit the doorbell and waited. In moments, the door opened. "Hello, Brevin," Ms. Revere said. "Thanks for those lovely flowers. Come on in!"

"Well," Brevin said, "when I was in the hospital you sent cards and came to visit me. That meant a lot."

Over coffee in Ms. Revere's living room, the teacher talked about the incident. "I was shaking like a leaf for days. I wasn't injured—but oh, man, I sure was spooked!"

"I felt really bad when I heard what happened to you," Brevin said. "Do you have any idea who did it?"

Ms. Revere shook her head. "I didn't think I had any enemies. The police searched for clues, but all they came up with was some bright bits of clunky jewelry. And that could have been something that one of the girls lost on Saturday morning," she said.

Brevin stared at the teacher. "What kind of jewelry?" he asked.

"Oh, some silly little carved thing that looked like it was made from an avocado pit. I guess it came off a necklace or a bracelet," Ms. Revere said.

Brevin suddenly remembered the soccer scholarship that Lucy had missed out on. "Uh—Ms. Revere," Brevin asked in a shaky voice, "do you remember when Lucy Arthur lost her eligibility to play soccer? Was it the failing grade in your science class that finally got her bounced off the team?"

She nodded. Then a look of sadness came over Ms. Revere's face. "That was one of the hardest grades I ever had to give—because I knew how much soccer meant to Lucy. But she wouldn't cooperate at all. There was no way I could avoid flunking her. I'm so sorry it cost her a shot at her dream. I tried so hard—" Ms. Revere said softly.

Brevin felt a great wave of relief wash over him. It was like a lead weight had suddenly been lifted from his shoulders. The doctors had warned him about irrational feelings of guilt. They said it was common with crime victims. That was *it!* Somehow, his confused, guilty feelings had been playing out in his nightmares. No *way* could he have hurt the teacher he so admired!

"Ms. Revere," he said, "is it okay with you if I use your phone to call the police? I think I know who attacked you. Let me explain . . ."